Also by Rachael Reed

Codefendant
Codefendant
Once a Cheater
Once a Cheater
Passport Bro
What Happens in Prison
Preference
Sprinkle Sprinkle
Championship Bad
Street Exodus
Street Exodus
Street Royalty
Pawns of Power
SIS
Cartel Bloodline
Get Money Girls
Skip the Games
Til Death Do Us Part
Backpage Hustle
Link in Bio
The Virgin and The Kingpin
A Gangsta's Heart
Boosters

Can't Turn a Hoe Into a Housewife

Championship
Bad

Rachael Reed
©2024

Check Out More Great Products and Free Giveaways
https://tbdbpublishing.com/

Despite it all, there was a spark in both Rochelle and Josh—a defiance against the odds stacked against them. They refused to be defined by their circumstances. They saw in each other a reflection of their own hopes and fears, a shared understanding of what it meant to fight for a better life.

As the sun set over the projects, casting long shadows over the cracked pavement, Rochelle and Josh stood side by side, looking out at their world. They didn't say much, but they didn't have to. In the silence, they found a sense of solidarity, a reminder that they weren't alone in their struggle.

"One day," Josh said quietly, "we're gonna get out of here. We're gonna make it."

Rochelle nodded, her eyes fixed on the horizon. "Yeah, one day."

But for now, they would keep fighting, keep dreaming, and keep surviving in the only way they knew how. The streets were tough, but so were they. And as long as they had their dreams, there was still a glimmer of hope amidst the darkness.

Chapter 2: Neighborhood Bonds

Rochelle and Josh's friendship was like a lifeline, a bond that had been forged in the fires of their shared struggles and mutual support. In the harsh reality of the Richmond housing projects, they found solace in each other, a refuge from the chaos that surrounded them.

Every morning, as Rochelle left for school, she would see Josh practicing his basketball moves on the cracked court outside their buildings. His determination was palpable, every jump shot, and every dribble a testament to his dreams of a better future.

"Yo, Rochelle!" Josh would call out, grinning as he effortlessly sank another basket. "You see that? They ain't ready for me!"

Rochelle would laugh, shaking her head. "You keep talkin', Josh. Just remember, actions speak louder than words."

Their friendship was a constant in an ever-changing world. They confided in each other about their fears, their dreams, and their frustrations. Rochelle would vent about the endless responsibilities she faced at home and school, while Josh would share his worries about his mother's addiction and the pressure to succeed.

One evening, as they sat on the steps of their building, watching the sunset paint the sky in hues of orange and pink, Josh turned to Rochelle with a serious expression. "You ever think about what it would be like to just get outta here? Leave all this behind?"

Rochelle sighed, her gaze distant. "Every damn day. But it's hard to see a way out when you're stuck in the middle of it."

Josh nodded, his eyes filled with determination. "I'm gonna make it, Rochelle. I swear. And when I do, I'm takin' you with me. We both deserve better."

As Josh's basketball career began to take off, his popularity soared. Talent scouts and college recruiters started showing up at his games, offering him glimpses of a life far removed from the projects. The attention was exhilarating, but it also brought new challenges.

"Man, you shoulda seen the look on their faces," Josh said excitedly after one game, where he had dominated the court. "They know I'm the real deal."

Rochelle was genuinely happy for him, but she couldn't help feeling a twinge of worry. "Those haters see you too, Josh. Stay focused and out the way."

But as Josh's star rose, so did the number of girls vying for his attention. They flocked to him, drawn by his charisma and the promise of his future success. Rochelle noticed the way they looked at him, the way they threw themselves at him, and it made her uneasy.

"What's the matter, Rochelle?" Josh teased one day, catching her eyeing one of his admirers with a frown. "You jealous?"

Rochelle scoffed, rolling her eyes. "Please, Josh. You ain't all that."

He laughed, nudging her playfully. "Oh, come on. You know you like me."

"Yeah, right," Rochelle shot back, though her heart did skip a beat. "Keep dreamin.'"

Despite her initial resistance, Rochelle couldn't deny the chemistry between them. Josh's playful flirting started to chip away at her defenses. He was persistent, always finding ways to make her laugh, to make her feel special.

One evening, after a particularly intense game, Josh found Rochelle waiting for him outside the gym. He was drenched in sweat, but his eyes lit up when he saw her. "What you doin' here?" he asked, surprised.

"Just wanted to see how you did," Rochelle replied, trying to sound casual.

Josh grinned, leaning in closer. "How 'bout you let me take you out sometime? Just you and me."

Rochelle hesitated, her heart pounding. She had always kept her guard up, afraid of getting hurt. But something about Josh made her want to take a chance. "Alright, Josh," she said finally, a smile tugging at her lips. "You get one shot. That's it, Don't mess it up."

Their friendship deepened as they started spending more time together. They would talk for hours, sharing their hopes and fears, dreaming of a future where they could leave the ghetto behind. Josh's success on the basketball court became a beacon of hope, not just for him, but for Rochelle as well.

As Josh continued to shine, the bond between them grew stronger. Rochelle found herself looking forward to their time together, the way his presence made her feel safe and cherished in a world that was often anything but.

But the streets were always watching, always waiting to pull them back into the darkness. For every moment of happiness, there was a lurking threat, a reminder of the harsh realities they faced. The projects were unforgiving, and their dreams were fragile.

One night, as they sat on the rooftop, looking out over the city, Josh took Rochelle's hand. "We're gonna make it out, Rochelle," he said, his voice filled with quiet determination. "No matter what, we're gonna find a way outta here."

Rochelle squeezed his hand, her heart filled with a mixture of hope and fear. "I believe you, Josh. I really do."

In that moment, they were more than just friends; they were partners in a shared dream, fighting against the odds to carve out a better future. The road ahead was uncertain, but as long as they had each other, they believed they could make it through anything.

The ghetto had shaped them, but it would not define them. Together, they would rise above the struggle, holding on to their dreams and each other, no matter how hard the journey.

Chapter 3: Giving In

The early morning sun filtered through the thin curtains of Rochelle's room, casting a soft glow on the walls adorned with dreams and aspirations. Today felt different. Today, Rochelle had decided to give in to the relentless pursuit of Josh, the boy next door whose persistence had worn down her defenses. She could no longer deny the chemistry between them, the way his smile made her heart race, or how his presence brought a sense of security in a world where safety was a luxury.

Later that day, Rochelle stood outside their building, nervously waiting for Josh. She watched him finish his usual morning basketball practice, his movements fluid and confident. As he jogged over, his face lit up with that trademark grin, she felt a mix of excitement and anxiety.

"Hey, Rochelle," Josh said, slightly out of breath but glowing with exhilaration from the game. "What's up? You look like you got somethin' on your mind."

Rochelle took a deep breath, gathering her courage. "Josh, I've been thinking... maybe we should give this a shot. You and me."

Josh's eyes widened in surprise, then softened with warmth. "For real? You serious?"

She nodded, feeling a shy smile spread across her face. "Yeah, I'm serious. Just... don't make me regret it."

Josh's grin widened as he stepped closer, his voice filled with genuine emotion. "You won't regret it, Rochelle. I promise."

Their relationship started with high hopes and mutual dreams of escaping the ghetto. They spent their days planning for a future where the harsh realities of their environment were mere memories.

Josh's basketball career seemed like the ticket out, and Rochelle's support was unwavering.

"One day, I'm gonna be playing in the big leagues," Josh would say, his eyes shining with determination. "And you'll be right there with me, cheering me on."

Rochelle would laugh, leaning into him. "Just don't forget about me when you're famous, Josh."

Their love was a beacon of light amidst the darkness of the projects. They found solace in each other, sharing moments of joy and tenderness that made their tough surroundings fade into the background. Josh would take Rochelle out on dates to places they could afford, like the local diner or a quiet spot by the river where they could dream without interruptions.

One evening, as they walked hand in hand through the neighborhood, Josh pulled her close. "You know, Rochelle, you make all this worth it. When I'm out there on the court, all I think about is you."

Rochelle smiled, feeling her heart swell with affection. "You better be thinking about that ball, Josh. I want you to win."

The excitement and newness of young love were intoxicating. They talked about their future, their plans to escape the ghetto and build a life together. Josh's basketball career seemed like a beacon of hope, a way to break free from the cycle of poverty and struggle.

But the ghetto life was never far behind. The streets were filled with dangers, and the challenges of their environment loomed large. The sound of gunshots was a constant reminder of the violence that surrounded them, and the police sirens were a nightly lullaby.

One night, as they sat on the steps of their building, Josh turned to Rochelle with a serious look in his eyes. "I need you to know,

Rochelle, that no matter what happens, I'm gonna take care of you. We're gonna get out of here."

Rochelle leaned her head on his shoulder, feeling the warmth of his promise. "I believe you, I believe you baby."

Their relationship was a source of strength for both of them, a refuge from the harsh realities of their world. They found joy in the small things, like sneaking into the local park after dark or sharing a stolen moment in the school hallway.

But even in their happiness, there were moments of tension. Josh's rising fame brought attention from other girls, and Rochelle couldn't help but feel a twinge of jealousy. She tried to brush it off, reminding herself that Josh had chosen her.

One afternoon, as they sat on a bench by the river, Rochelle voiced her fears. "Josh, promise me something. Promise me you won't let all this attention get to your head."

Josh looked at her, his expression serious. "I promise, Rochelle. You're the one I want. None of that other stuff matters."

Their love was a delicate balance between the dreams they shared and the reality they lived in. The streets were unforgiving, but as long as they had each other, they believed they could conquer anything. Together, they faced the challenges of their environment, holding on to their dreams and each other, determined to find a way out.

The excitement of young love gave them hope, a belief that despite the odds, they could rise above the struggles of their surroundings. And as they navigated the twists and turns of their relationship, they clung to the promise of a brighter future, where their dreams could finally become reality.

Chapter 4: Rising Star

Josh's rise to fame was swift and dazzling. His name echoed through the halls of Richmond High and beyond, carried on the breath of talent scouts and college recruiters. Every game he played was a testament to his raw talent and unyielding determination, and the local community watched in awe as one of their own began to shine so brightly.

"Yo, Josh, you gonna make it to the NBA, man!" his friends would shout after a game, their voices filled with genuine admiration and a tinge of envy. Josh would smile, his confidence bolstered by the cheers and the attention. But behind that smile, he felt the weight of their expectations and the mounting pressures of his rising fame.

For Rochelle, watching Josh's ascent was both exhilarating and nerve-wracking. She was proud of him, no doubt. Seeing him dominate the court, hearing his name spoken with such reverence, filled her with a pride that warmed her heart. But with every cheer, with every new face that turned his way, there was a flicker of insecurity that she couldn't shake.

One evening, after another stellar performance, Rochelle waited for Josh outside the gym. He emerged, surrounded by a throng of admirers, laughing and basking in the glow of his victory. As he spotted her, his face lit up, and he made his way through the crowd.

"Hey, baby," he said, pulling her into a tight hug. "You see that game? We killed it out there!"

"I saw," Rochelle replied, her smile genuine but her eyes betraying a hint of worry. "You were amazing, Josh. Everyone's talking about you."

Josh grinned, clearly enjoying the attention. "Yeah, it's crazy, right? Talent scouts from UVA and Duke were here tonight. They wanna talk about scholarships."

Rochelle's heart swelled with pride, but the insecurities gnawed at her. "That's great, Josh. Really. Just...don't forget about us, okay?"

He pulled back slightly, looking her in the eyes. "I could never forget about you, Rochelle. You're my number one. Always."

Despite his assurances, Rochelle couldn't help but notice the growing number of girls who flocked to Josh after every game. They giggled and flirted, batting their eyelashes and vying for his attention. It made her stomach churn with jealousy and fear. She tried to trust Josh, but the constant competition was right in her face regularly and they didn't care one bit.

As Josh's fame grew, so did the temptations. Parties, offers, and the allure of a life beyond the ghetto started to seep into his world. Talent scouts and college recruiters promised him the moon, and the local community hailed him as their golden boy, the one who could make it out and put Richmond on the map.

But with these promises came pressures. Josh felt the weight of his family's hopes, his friends' expectations, and the community's dreams resting on his shoulders. The late-night parties, the drugs, and the endless stream of admirers were temptations that threatened to derail his focus.

One night, as he and Rochelle sat on the steps of their building, Josh confided in her. "It's a lot, Rochelle. Sometimes, I feel like I'm being pulled in a million different directions. Everyone wants something from me."

Rochelle took his hand, her voice gentle but firm. "You gotta stay focused, Josh. Remember why you're doing this. Don't let the hype get to your head."

Josh nodded, squeezing her hand. "I know, baby. It's just...it's hard. I don't wanna mess this up."

Rochelle's pride in Josh's achievements was undeniable, but her insecurities lingered. She feared that as he climbed higher, he might outgrow their relationship. The attention he received from other girls only fueled her worries.

One afternoon, after practice, Rochelle overheard a group of girls talking about Josh. "Did you see the way he looked at me?" one of them gushed. "I swear, he's into me."

Rochelle felt a pang of anger. She wanted to march over and set the record straight, but she knew that would only make things worse. Instead, she kept her head high and walked past them, reminding herself that Josh was hers and they had made a promise to each other.

The pressure was not only on Josh but on their relationship as well. They had to navigate the minefield of fame and temptation while keeping their bond strong. Rochelle supported Josh wholeheartedly, but she couldn't ignore the nagging doubts that crept into her mind.

As the season progressed, Josh's talent continued to shine, and the offers from colleges became more concrete. He was on the brink of something incredible, something that could change their lives forever. But with each step forward, the challenges grew more daunting.

One evening, after a particularly intense game, Josh sat with Rochelle by the river. The moonlight reflected off the water, casting a serene glow over them. "You know, sometimes I wonder if I'm ready for all this," he admitted, his voice tinged with vulnerability.

Rochelle looked at him, her eyes filled with love and determination. "You are, Josh. You've worked so hard for this. Just remember why you started."

Josh smiled, pulling her close. "I know, Rochelle. And I'm grateful for you every day. We're gonna make it, together."

Their journey was far from over, and the road ahead was fraught with challenges. But as long as they had each other, they believed they could navigate the twists and turns of Josh's rising fame. Together, they faced the temptations and pressures, holding on to their dreams and the love that had brought them this far. The streets of Richmond were tough, but so were they. And as long as they stayed true to each other, they believed they could conquer anything.

Chapter 5: Infidelity and Betrayal

The signs were subtle at first. Josh's phone buzzing more frequently, his attention diverted by an endless stream of texts and social media notifications. Rochelle tried to ignore the nagging doubts, telling herself that the attention was just part of Josh's rising fame. But as the days passed, those doubts grew harder to dismiss.

One evening, Rochelle sat in her room, scrolling through her phone when a message popped up from a girl she vaguely recognized from Josh's games. The message was blunt and painful: "I saw Josh with another girl last night. Thought you should know."

Rochelle's heart pounded as she read the message over and over, each word like a dagger to her chest. She felt a mix of anger, betrayal, and a sinking feeling of dread. She had always feared this moment, but seeing it confirmed was something else entirely.

Later that night, when Josh came over, Rochelle confronted him. "Josh, we need to talk."

Josh looked at her, sensing the tension in her voice. "What's wrong, Rochelle?"

She took a deep breath, trying to keep her voice steady. "I got a message today. Someone said they saw you with another girl. Is it true?"

Josh's eyes widened, and he immediately went on the defensive. "Who told you that? They're lying, Rochelle. You know you're the only one for me."

Rochelle's anger flared. "Don't lie to me, Josh. I've seen the way you act around those girls. I'm not stupid."

The argument escalated quickly, voices rising, and emotions running high. "You think I'm out here risking everything for some random girl?" Josh shouted. "I'm doing this for us!"

"For us? Or for you and your ego?" Rochelle shot back, her voice breaking with emotion. "I thought we were in this together, Josh. How could you do this to me?"

Josh's face hardened, his pride stinging. "You don't understand the pressure I'm under. Everyone wants something from me. Sometimes I just...I need to escape."

Rochelle's eyes filled with tears, the betrayal cutting deep. "And you escape by cheating on me? Is that it?"

The confrontation was raw and intense, the kind that only young love could produce. Emotions were laid bare, and the pain was palpable. They argued late into the night, neither willing to back down, each word a blow to their already fragile relationship.

The fight ended with Josh storming out, slamming the door behind him. Rochelle collapsed onto her bed, sobbing into her pillow. The betrayal was like a wound, fresh and bleeding, and she couldn't see a way to heal it.

Over the next few days, Rochelle tried to focus on her schoolwork and responsibilities at home, but the fight with Josh loomed over her like a dark cloud. She couldn't escape the whispers and knowing looks from people in the neighborhood. Gossip spread quickly, and everyone seemed to have an opinion on their relationship.

One afternoon, as Rochelle was walking home, she ran into Josh's best friend, Darnell. He gave her a sympathetic look. "Rochelle, you okay? Heard about the fight."

Rochelle sighed, feeling the weight of everyone's eyes on her. "I don't know, Darnell. I'm just...I'm trying to figure things out."

Darnell nodded, understanding. "Josh is messed up over it too. But you gotta know, this life ain't easy. Temptations are everywhere."

Rochelle's anger flared again. "That's not an excuse, Darnell. He made a choice. He chose to hurt me."

Darnell put a hand on her shoulder. "I get it. Just...don't give up on him yet. He needs you."

Rochelle walked away, her mind a whirlwind of emotions. She loved Josh, but the betrayal had cut deep. She wasn't sure if their relationship could survive this, and the thought of losing him was almost as painful as the infidelity itself.

That night, as she lay in bed, Rochelle replayed the fight in her mind. The words, the accusations, the hurt—it all felt so fresh. She knew they needed to talk, to figure out where they stood, but the thought of facing Josh again filled her with dread.

The next day, Josh showed up at her door, looking exhausted and remorseful. "Rochelle, can we talk?"

She hesitated, then nodded, letting him in. They sat in the living room, the silence heavy between them.

"I messed up," Josh said finally, his voice filled with regret. "I let the fame get to me, and I hurt you. I'm so sorry, Rochelle."

Rochelle looked at him, her eyes still red from crying. "I don't know if I can trust you again, Josh. How do I know you won't do this again?"

Josh reached for her hand, his touch hesitant. "I'll do anything to make it right. I love you, Rochelle. I can't lose you."

The sincerity in his voice tugged at her heart, but the pain of betrayal was still fresh. "It's gonna take time, Josh. We can't just pretend this didn't happen."

He nodded, tears welling in his eyes. "I know. And I'm willing to do whatever it takes. Just give me a chance."

Rochelle sighed, feeling the weight of their relationship on her shoulders. "Alright, Josh. But you need to prove it. Actions speak louder than words."

Josh squeezed her hand, a flicker of hope in his eyes. "I will, Rochelle. I promise."

As they sat together, the rawness of their emotions slowly giving way to a tentative hope, Rochelle realized that their journey was far from over. The streets of Richmond were tough, but so were they. And as long as they faced the challenges together, there was still a chance for them to find their way back to each other.

Chapter 6: Gossip and Scandal

The Richmond housing projects were alive with whispers, and it didn't take long for news of Josh's infidelity to spread like wildfire. Everywhere Rochelle went, she could feel the eyes on her, hear the hushed conversations that would abruptly stop when she walked by. The streets thrived on gossip, and right now, she was the main topic.

Rochelle kept her head down as she walked to school, her shoulders hunched against the weight of the stares. It seemed like everyone had something to say about her and Josh. The he said, she said drama was relentless, and the scrutiny was suffocating.

"Hey, Rochelle," a girl called out as she passed a group of students. "Is it true you and Josh broke up and he is with somebody else now?"

Rochelle clenched her jaw, refusing to engage. She didn't owe anyone an explanation, but the constant barrage of questions and comments chipped away at her resolve.

At school, the whispers followed her. In the hallways, in the classrooms, even in the bathrooms—there was no escape. The rumor mill churned out stories faster than she could keep up, each one more sensational than the last.

"You hear about Josh and that girl on the cheer squad?" one student said, not noticing Rochelle nearby.

"Yeah, I heard they were together now," another replied, their voices dripping with scandal.

Rochelle's stomach turned. She wanted to scream, to tell them all to mind their own business, but she knew that would only fuel the fire. Instead, she took a deep breath and focused on getting through the day.

During lunch, Rochelle sat alone, picking at her food. She was tired of the constant judgment, the sideways glances, and the pitying looks. It felt like the whole world was watching her fall apart.

"Hey, Rochelle," came a voice she recognized. It was Tonya, a girl from the neighborhood who had always been friendly. "Mind if I sit with you?"

Rochelle shrugged, grateful for the company. "Sure, go ahead."

Tonya sat down, giving Rochelle a sympathetic smile. "I heard about what happened with Josh. I'm really sorry you're going through this."

"Thanks," Rochelle mumbled, not sure what else to say.

Tonya leaned in closer, her voice dropping to a conspiratorial whisper. "You know, people are gonna talk no matter what. But I'm here for you. If you need anything, just let me know."

Rochelle nodded, feeling a small measure of comfort. It was nice to have someone on her side, or so she thought. What Rochelle didn't realize was that Tonya had her own motives for getting close. She had always been jealous of Rochelle's relationship with Josh and saw this as an opportunity to stir the pot.

Over the next few days, Tonya made a point of being there for Rochelle, offering a listening ear and words of support. "You deserve better, Rochelle. Josh doesn't appreciate what he has."

Rochelle appreciated the sentiment, but she couldn't shake the feeling that something was off. It was only when she overheard Tonya talking to another girl that her suspicions were confirmed.

"I'm just saying, if Rochelle can't keep her man in check, maybe someone else should step in," Tonya said, her voice dripping with false concern.

Rochelle's blood boiled. She felt betrayed and humiliated all over again. It wasn't enough that she had to deal with Josh's cheating and the public scrutiny—now she had to watch her back around someone she thought was a friend.

Confronting Tonya was inevitable. Rochelle found her after school, leaning against a wall with a group of girls, clearly enjoying the attention.

"Tonya," Rochelle called out, her voice hard. "We need to talk."

Tonya turned, a smirk playing on her lips. "What's up, Rochelle?"

Rochelle stepped closer, her eyes blazing with anger. "I heard what you said. You're not my friend. You're just using this to get closer to Josh."

Tonya's smirk faltered, but she quickly recovered. "Oh, come on, Rochelle. Don't be so dramatic. I was just looking out for you."

"Looking out for me?" Rochelle scoffed. "You're spreading rumors and trying to take advantage of the situation. Stay out of my business, Tonya."

Tonya shrugged, her eyes cold. "Fine. But don't say I didn't try to help."

Rochelle walked away, her heart pounding. The confrontation had left her feeling more isolated than ever. She realized that in the world of the projects, trust was a rare commodity, and she couldn't afford to be careless with it.

As the days passed, Rochelle did her best to ignore the gossip and focus on herself. She threw herself into her schoolwork and helped her mom around the house, anything to keep her mind off the drama. She also kept her distance from Josh, needing time to figure out if their relationship was worth saving.

One evening, as she was walking home, she saw Josh waiting for her outside her building. He looked tired and worn, his usual confidence replaced by a weary vulnerability.

"Rochelle, can we talk?" he asked, his voice low.

Rochelle hesitated, then nodded. "Okay."

They sat on the steps, the cool evening air wrapping around them like a shroud. "I know I messed up," Josh began, his voice filled with regret. "And I know everyone's talking about us. But I still love you, Rochelle. I'm willing to do whatever it takes to make things right."

Rochelle looked at him, her heart torn. "I don't know, Josh. It's not just about what you did. It's about the trust we lost. Can we really get that back?"

Josh reached for her hand, his touch tentative. "We can try. I'm not giving up on us."

As they sat together, the weight of their situation pressing down on them, Rochelle realized that their journey was far from over. The streets of Richmond were filled with challenges, but she was determined to navigate them with strength and resilience. Whether their relationship would survive was uncertain, but one thing was clear: Rochelle would face whatever came next with her head held high.

Chapter 7: The Cycle of Violence

The tension between Rochelle and Josh was palpable. The once-loving relationship had become a battlefield, where every conversation seemed to lead to a fight. The cycle of arguing, making up, and then arguing again intensified, and each round took a heavier toll on both of them.

It began with harsh words, accusations thrown like daggers. The arguments often started over small things—an innocent comment taken the wrong way, a glance that lingered too long on someone else, or a perceived slight. But the underlying issues of trust and betrayal always lurked beneath the surface, ready to explode at any moment.

"Where were you last night?" Rochelle demanded one evening, her voice trembling with anger.

"I told you, I was with Darnell," Josh replied, his tone defensive.

"Yeah, and I'm supposed to believe that? After everything that's happened?" Rochelle's eyes flashed with hurt and fury.

Josh clenched his fists, his temper flaring. "Why can't you just trust me for once?"

"Trust you? After you cheated on me? You expect me to just forget about that?" Rochelle's voice was rising, her emotions boiling over.

The argument escalated, their voices echoing through the thin walls of their apartment building. Neighbors could hear the shouting and the slamming doors, but no one intervened. In the projects, people learned to mind their own business.

As the fights grew more intense, so did the physical altercations. One night, during a particularly heated argument, Josh grabbed

Rochelle's arm, his grip tight and unforgiving. "Let go of me, Josh!" she yelled, struggling to free herself.

"Why do you always have to push me?" he shouted back, his eyes wild with anger. "Why can't you just let it go?"

Rochelle managed to break free, shoving him away. "You don't own me, Josh! You can't control me like that!"

The violence was sporadic but devastating. Each incident left both of them emotionally and physically scarred, further damaging their already fragile relationship. The impact on their mental health was profound. Rochelle found herself feeling constantly on edge, unable to sleep or focus on her schoolwork. The stress was affecting her in ways she couldn't fully comprehend.

Josh, too, was struggling. The pressure of his basketball career, combined with the volatility of his relationship with Rochelle, was taking a toll on his performance on the court. He started missing shots he would normally make with ease, and his frustration grew.

Their friends noticed the changes but felt powerless to help. Darnell tried to talk to Josh, urging him to take a step back and think about what he was doing. "Man, you need to chill. This ain't healthy for either of you."

Josh ran a hand through his hair, sighing heavily. "I know, Darnell. But I love her. I just... I don't know how to fix this."

Rochelle confided in her friend Keisha, who listened with a mix of concern and frustration. "Girl, you need to get out of this mess. It's not worth it."

Rochelle's eyes filled with tears. "I know, Keisha. But I love him. And I keep hoping things will get better."

The cycle of violence and reconciliation continued, each round leaving deeper wounds. They would have explosive fights, followed by tearful apologies and passionate makeups. In those moments of reconciliation, they clung to the hope that things could change, that their love could overcome the darkness that had crept into their lives.

But the reality was stark and unforgiving. The physical altercations became more frequent, and the emotional toll more severe. Rochelle started to question her own worth, wondering if she deserved better or if this was her fate.

One night, after another brutal argument that ended with Rochelle nursing a bruised wrist, she sat alone in her room, the weight of her situation pressing down on her. She thought about her mother, who had sacrificed so much to raise her, and how disappointed she would be to see her daughter caught in such a destructive relationship.

Rochelle knew she had to make a change, but the thought of leaving Josh was almost as painful as staying. She loved him, despite everything, and the idea of a life without him was terrifying. But she also knew that the violence was tearing them both apart, and if they didn't break the cycle, it would destroy them.

The streets of Richmond were unforgiving, and the pressures of their environment only intensified the struggles they faced. In the darkness of her room, Rochelle made a decision. She would confront Josh, not with anger, but with a plea for them to seek help, to find a way to heal the wounds they had inflicted on each other.

The next day, Rochelle approached Josh with a mixture of determination and fear. "Josh, can we talk?" she said, her voice trembling.

He looked at her, his eyes weary and sad. "Yeah, we can."

As they sat down to talk, Rochelle hoped that this conversation would be different, that it would mark the beginning of a new chapter for them. They needed to break the cycle, to find a way to heal and move forward. It wouldn't be easy, but it was their only chance at saving their relationship and their sanity.

In the unforgiving world of the projects, love and violence were often intertwined, but Rochelle was determined to find a way to separate them. She owed it to herself and to Josh to try, even if the odds were stacked against them.

Chapter 8: Pressure Cooker

As the days counted down to the championship game, the atmosphere in Richmond was electric. Josh's name was on everyone's lips, and the whole neighborhood buzzed with anticipation. This game was more than just a match; it was a potential ticket out of the projects, a chance for Josh to secure a future far removed from the struggles that had defined his life.

For Josh, the pressure was immense. Every practice, every moment on the court, carried the weight of expectation. Talent scouts from top colleges were planning to attend, and the community was looking to him as the one that would make it out. His coach drilled him harder, teammates looked to him for leadership, and his family pinned their dreams on his success.

Rochelle watched all this unfold with a mix of pride and trepidation. She had always believed in Josh, but as his star rose, she felt herself increasingly pushed to the sidelines. Their relationship, already strained, seemed to be fraying further as Josh's ambitions consumed him.

One evening, as Josh returned home from a grueling practice, Rochelle tried to talk to him. "Josh, you've been so busy. We barely see each other anymore."

He looked at her, exhaustion and frustration etched on his face. "I know, Rochelle. But this game... it's everything. I need to focus."

"I get that," Rochelle replied, struggling to keep her voice steady. "But it feels like you're not even trying to work on this. We need to find time for us."

Josh sighed, rubbing his temples. "Can we not do this right now? I'm tired. We'll talk after the game, okay?"

Rochelle nodded, feeling a pang of hurt. "Sure, after the game."

As the days passed, the distance between them grew. Josh was always at practice or meetings, and when he was home, he was too exhausted to talk. Rochelle tried to focus on her own dreams, but it was hard not to feel sidelined by Josh's relentless pursuit of his goals.

One afternoon, while Rochelle was at the store, she overheard some customers discussing Josh's upcoming game. "You think he'll make it big?" one of them asked.

"Definitely," another replied. "But I wonder what'll happen with Rochelle. She's a good girl, but that life you know the athlete wife life... it's not easy."

Rochelle's heart sank. She knew they were right. The pressures of their environment, combined with Josh's ambitions, were creating a rift that seemed impossible to bridge.

As the championship game approached, tensions reached a boiling point. Josh was more stressed than ever, and Rochelle felt increasingly isolated. Their conversations turned into arguments, each one more intense than the last.

"Josh, you promised we'd talk," Rochelle said one night, her voice trembling with frustration.

"I know, but I can't deal with this right now!" Josh snapped. "The game is in two days. Can't you understand how important this is?"

"Of course, I do! But you're shutting me out. It's like you don't care about us anymore," Rochelle shot back, tears welling up in her eyes.

Josh looked at her, his expression softening for a moment. "I do care, Rochelle. But this game... it's our way out. I'm doing this for us."

"Then show me," Rochelle pleaded. "Show me that we still matter."

The argument ended with Josh storming out, slamming the door behind him. Rochelle collapsed onto the couch, feeling a mix of anger, sadness, and fear. She loved Josh, but the pressure was tearing them apart.

The night before the championship game, Josh stayed out late, trying to clear his head. He wandered the streets, replaying their arguments in his mind. He knew Rochelle was right, but he felt trapped by the expectations placed upon him.

Rochelle, meanwhile, lay awake in bed, her mind racing. She knew Josh was under immense pressure, but so was she. Their relationship was crumbling, and she didn't know how to fix it.

The day of the game arrived, and the entire neighborhood turned out to support Josh. The gym was packed, the air thick with anticipation. Rochelle sat in the front row, her heart pounding as she watched Josh warm up on the court.

As the game began, Josh played with a ferocity that left the crowd in awe. He made shot after shot, his focus unyielding. But Rochelle could see the strain in his eyes, the weight of the pressure bearing down on him.

At halftime, Josh's team was ahead, but the tension was strong. Rochelle made her way to the locker room, hoping to offer him some support. She found him sitting alone, his head in his hands.

"Josh," she said softly, sitting next to him. "You're doing great. Just... remember why you're doing this."

He looked up at her, his eyes filled with exhaustion and determination. "I know. For us."

But the second half of the game was brutal. The opposing team fought back hard, and the pressure mounted. Josh pushed himself to the limit, but a bad fall left him clutching his leg in pain. The gym fell silent as he was helped off the court, his face contorted in agony.

Rochelle's heart shattered as she watched him, the weight of their struggles crashing down on her. The game ended in a narrow defeat, and the crowd dispersed, leaving Josh and Rochelle to face the aftermath alone.

As they sat together in the empty gym, Rochelle held Josh's hand, tears streaming down her face. "We'll get through this," she whispered, her voice breaking. "We have to."

Josh nodded, his own tears falling. "I know, Rochelle. I'm so sorry."

In that moment, they both realized that the pressures of their environment and their own ambitions had nearly destroyed them. But they also knew that their love was worth fighting for. They would have to find a way to rebuild, to heal the wounds inflicted by their dreams and the harsh realities of the streets.

As they walked home together, leaning on each other for support, Rochelle and Josh knew that their journey was far from over. The road ahead would be difficult, but as long as they faced it together, they believed they could overcome anything. The streets of Richmond were tough, but so were they, and their love would guide them through the darkest of times.

Chapter 9: The Breaking Point

The streets were unusually quiet this night, the stillness only amplifying the tension simmering between Rochelle and Josh. They had been circling each other for days, the weight of their unspoken grievances growing heavier with each passing moment. Tonight, the dam would finally break.

Josh had come home late again, his eyes red and his demeanor defensive. Rochelle had heard the whispers, seen the texts, and the rumors had now solidified into painful reality. As Josh stumbled through the door, Rochelle confronted him, her voice shaking with barely controlled fury.

"Where the hell have you been, Josh?" Rochelle demanded, her hands trembling. "You think I don't know? You think I'm stupid?"

Josh slumped against the wall, his face a mask of exhaustion and guilt. "Rochelle, please. I don't want to do this right now."

"Oh, we're doing this!" Rochelle's voice rose, each word slicing through the air like a knife. "Who is she this time? Another girl from the cheer team? Or is it someone new?"

Josh's eyes flickered with anger, his own temper flaring. "I told you, it's nothing. You're blowing this out of proportion."

"Blowing it out of proportion?" Rochelle's voice cracked with emotion. "I'm carrying your child, Josh! How could you do this to us?"

The mention of the baby was a gut punch, and Josh recoiled, his face contorting with a mix of shame and anger. "Rochelle, I didn't mean for any of this to happen. You don't understand the pressure I'm under."

"The pressure you're under?" Rochelle stepped closer, her fists clenched. "What about me? What about our baby?"

The argument escalated rapidly, their voices rising to a fever pitch. Harsh words were exchanged, each one cutting deeper than the last. Rochelle's rage was fueled by a cocktail of betrayal, fear, and heartbreak, while Josh's defenses crumbled under the weight of his own guilt.

"You're a selfish bastard, Josh!" Rochelle screamed, shoving him hard.

Josh stumbled back, losing his balance. He crashed into a table, a sharp pain shooting through his leg as he fell to the floor. The impact was brutal, and he cried out in agony, clutching his leg.

Rochelle froze, her anger dissipating in an instant as she realized what had happened. "Josh! Oh my God, are you okay?"

But Josh's pain quickly turned to rage. He pushed himself up, his face twisted in fury. "You did this to me! You ruined everything!" he shouted, lunging at her.

In the chaos, Rochelle tried to defend herself, but Josh's strength and anger overwhelmed her. He shoved her hard, and she fell backward, hitting her head against the corner of a table. Pain exploded in her skull, and darkness began to creep into the edges of her vision.

As she lay there, struggling to stay conscious, the full horror of the situation washed over her. She felt a sharp, unbearable pain in her abdomen, and instinctively knew something was terribly wrong. Her vision blurred, and the last thing she saw was Josh's anguished face before everything went black.

When Rochelle woke up, she was in a hospital bed, the sterile smell of disinfectant filling her nostrils. The room was dimly lit, and her body felt heavy, every movement a struggle. She tried to sit up, but a wave of pain and dizziness forced her back down.

A nurse entered the room, her expression gentle but serious. "Rochelle, you're awake. How are you feeling?"

Rochelle's voice was weak, barely a whisper. "What happened? Where's Josh?"

The nurse hesitated, then sighed. "You were brought in unconscious. You've suffered a concussion and... I'm so sorry, Rochelle, but you had a miscarriage."

The words hit Rochelle like a sledgehammer, knocking the breath out of her. Tears welled up in her eyes, and she turned her face away, unable to process the magnitude of her loss. She had known, deep down, but hearing it confirmed was devastating.

"Is Josh... is he here?" she asked, her voice cracking.

The nurse shook her head. "He was treated for a leg injury and left shortly after. He said he needed some time."

Rochelle's heart shattered into a million pieces. Not only had she lost their baby, but she was facing this trauma alone. The betrayal, the fight, the miscarriage—it was all too much to bear.

She lay back against the pillows, tears streaming down her face. The pain in her heart was far worse than any physical injury. She had trusted Josh, believed in their future, and now it was all crumbling around her.

As she stared at the ceiling, Rochelle made a silent vow. She would find the strength to get through this, to rebuild her life, even if it meant doing it without Josh. The streets of Richmond had taken so much from her, but they would not take her spirit.

The road ahead would be long and filled with challenges, but Rochelle was determined to rise above the pain and loss. She would find a way to heal, to reclaim her dreams, and to forge a future that was truly her own. The streets were unforgiving, but so was her resolve, and she would not let this be the end of her story.

Chapter 10: Heartbreak and Betrayal

Rochelle lay in the hospital bed, her body aching from the physical and emotional trauma. The sterile, white walls of the room seemed to close in on her, amplifying the loneliness and pain that gnawed at her soul. Each breath felt like a struggle, a reminder of the violence that had shattered her life and stolen her baby.

The nurses came and went, their faces kind but detached, their words meant to comfort but falling flat. Rochelle's mother visited often, her eyes filled with worry and sadness, but also with a strength that Rochelle struggled to summon within herself.

"Baby, you're gonna be okay," her mother would say, holding her hand. "You're strong. Stronger than you know."

Rochelle would nod, trying to believe those words, but the betrayal and loss weighed heavily on her heart. She had trusted Josh, loved him with everything she had, and he had thrown it all away. The memory of their last fight haunted her, the rawness of his anger and her own helplessness replaying in her mind.

It had been a few days, and slowly, Rochelle began to recover physically. The bruises faded, the cuts healed, but the emotional scars remained raw and painful. Each time she closed her eyes, she saw Josh's face twisted in rage, felt the sharp pang of loss in her abdomen.

One afternoon, as Rochelle sat in the hospital garden trying to find a moment of peace, her friend Keisha visited. Keisha had been a constant source of support, always checking in, always offering a shoulder to cry on.

"How you holding up, girl?" Keisha asked, sitting beside Rochelle and handing her a small bouquet of flowers.

Rochelle managed a weak smile. "I'm getting there. It's just... a lot, you know?"

Keisha nodded, her expression sympathetic. "I know. But you're tough, Rochelle. You'll get through this."

They talked for a while, the conversation a welcome distraction from Rochelle's thoughts. But as Keisha prepared to leave, she hesitated, a troubled look crossing her face.

"Rochelle, there's something you need to know," Keisha said, her voice tense.

Rochelle's heart skipped a beat. "What is it?"

"It's about Josh," Keisha began, her eyes flicking away. "He's... he's been seeing someone else. Even while you've been in here."

Rochelle felt a cold knot of dread form in her stomach. "Who?"

Keisha took a deep breath. "Tonya."

The name hit Rochelle like a slap. Tonya, who had pretended to be her friend, who had offered fake sympathy while secretly coveting Josh. The betrayal cut deep, reopening wounds that had barely begun to heal.

"Are you sure?" Rochelle asked, her voice barely a whisper.

Keisha nodded, her eyes filled with sorrow. "I'm so sorry, Rochelle. I thought you should know."

Rochelle felt a wave of anger and sadness crash over her. She had believed in Josh, even after everything, and he had continued to betray her. The realization of her own vulnerability, of how completely she had been deceived, was almost too much to bear.

Later that night, alone in her hospital room, Rochelle let the tears flow freely. She cried for her lost baby, for the love she had given so freely, for the trust that had been shattered. She cried until there were no more tears left, only a hollow ache in her chest.

The next day, determined to confront the truth, Rochelle called Josh. He answered on the third ring, his voice cautious. "Rochelle?"

"We need to talk," she said, her voice steady but cold. "Face to face."

Josh hesitated, then agreed. They met in the hospital garden, the place where Rochelle had tried to find solace. Josh limped slightly, his injured leg a reminder of the violence that had erupted between them.

"Rochelle, I'm so sorry," Josh began, his eyes filled with regret.

Rochelle held up a hand, stopping him. "I know about Tonya."

Josh's face paled, guilt written all over his features. "Rochelle, I..."

"How could you?" Rochelle's voice cracked with pain. "After everything we've been through, after losing our baby, how could you do this to me?"

Josh looked down, unable to meet her gaze. "I messed up. I'm sorry. I didn't mean to hurt you."

Rochelle laughed bitterly. "You didn't mean to hurt me? You are tryna destroy me, Josh. You are tryna destroy us."

The confrontation was raw and painful, but it also brought a sense of closure. Rochelle realized that the Josh she had loved was gone, replaced by someone she no longer recognized. The betrayal had cut too deep, and there was no going back.

"I can't do this anymore, Josh," Rochelle said, her voice steady. "We're done."

Josh's eyes filled with tears, but he nodded, accepting her decision. "I'm so sorry, Rochelle. I hope you find happiness."

Rochelle watched him leave, a mixture of sadness and relief washing over her. She had loved him, but love wasn't enough to heal the wounds he had inflicted. It was time to move on, to find her own strength and rebuild her life.

As she walked back to her room, Rochelle felt a newfound determination. She had been through hell, but she had survived. The streets of Richmond were tough, but she was tougher. And she would find a way to rise above the pain, to reclaim her dreams and her future.

The journey ahead would be difficult, but Rochelle was ready. She had faced betrayal and heartbreak and come out stronger. Now it was time to take control of her life and build a future on her own terms.

Chapter 11: The Fallout

The air in the Richmond housing projects was thick with tension and gossip. The fight between Josh and Rochelle had not only shattered their relationship but had also sent shockwaves through the community. Josh's basketball dreams lay in ruins, and Rochelle was grappling with her personal loss and the harsh new reality that had been thrust upon her.

Josh limped down the cracked sidewalks, his leg in a brace, the pain a constant reminder of the night everything fell apart. His future in basketball, once so bright, now seemed distant and unreachable. The scouts and recruiters who had once shown interest had all but disappeared, their hopes for his potential dashed by the injury and the scandal.

"Yo, Josh! What happened, man?" A group of boys called out as he passed, their tones a mix of curiosity and disappointment. The news had spread quickly: the golden boy of Richmond High had fallen.

Josh forced a smile, but it didn't reach his eyes. "Just messed up, you know. Life happens."

The boys nodded, but Josh could feel their judgment. The streets had a way of turning on you when you fell from grace. He knew they were talking about him behind his back, dissecting his failures, and speculating about his future—or lack thereof.

Meanwhile, Rochelle was trying to find her footing in the aftermath of the fight. The miscarriage had left a gaping wound in her heart, and the betrayal by Josh and Tonya had shattered her trust in those around her. The community's reaction was a cacophony of voices, some offering support, others condemning her.

"Did you hear about Rochelle? Lost the baby and dumped Josh. Can you believe it?"

"She should've seen it coming. Josh was never gonna settle down. Too much pressure for a young man."

"Poor girl. She's been through so much. Hope she can bounce back."

Rochelle overheard these snippets of conversation as she walked to the corner store, each comment cutting deeper than the last. She felt like a spectacle, her pain laid bare for everyone to scrutinize. The judgment stung, but what hurt more was the mix of pity and gossip that followed her everywhere she went.

At the store, Mrs. Jenkins, the owner, gave her a sympathetic look. "How you holding up, Rochelle?"

Rochelle forced a smile. "I'm managing, Mrs. Jenkins. Just taking it one day at a time."

Mrs. Jenkins nodded, her eyes soft with understanding. "If you need anything, you let me know, alright? You're stronger than you think."

Rochelle thanked her and quickly left, the weight of everyone's eyes on her shoulders. She needed to get away, to find a place where she could breathe without feeling judged or pitied. She made her way to the small park at the edge of the projects, a place where she and Josh used to dream about a better future.

Sitting on a worn bench, Rochelle let the tears flow freely. She cried for her lost baby, for the love she had given so freely, for the dreams that had been snatched away. The grief was overwhelming, and for a moment, she felt like she was drowning in it.

But as the tears subsided, a sense of clarity began to emerge. She couldn't change the past, couldn't undo the pain and betrayal, but she could choose how to move forward. She had survived so much already, and she knew she had the strength to rebuild her life, even if it meant doing it alone.

Over the next few weeks, Rochelle focused on her recovery, both physical and emotional. She went back to school, determined to finish her education and create a future for herself. She avoided Josh and Tonya, refusing to let their betrayal define her.

The community's reaction remained mixed. Some people continued to gossip and judge, while others offered quiet support. Rochelle learned to tune out the negativity, focusing instead on the small acts of kindness that reminded her she wasn't completely alone.

One day, as she walked to school, she ran into Darnell, Josh's best friend. He looked at her with a mixture of regret and sorrow. "Rochelle, I'm really sorry about everything. Josh... he messed up big time."

Rochelle nodded, her expression calm but distant. "Thanks, Darnell. But I'm moving on. I can't let this hold me back."

Darnell nodded, respect in his eyes. "You're strong, Rochelle. Stronger than most people I know."

Rochelle managed a small smile. "I have to be."

The streets of Richmond were harsh and unforgiving, but Rochelle had learned to navigate them with resilience and determination. She would not let the fallout from her relationship with Josh define her. Instead, she would use it as a stepping stone, a reminder of her own strength and the lessons she had learned.

As she walked away, Rochelle felt a renewed sense of purpose. She had been through the fire and come out the other side, stronger and more determined than ever. The road ahead would be challenging, but she was ready to face it, one step at a time. The streets might be tough, but Rochelle was tougher, and she would forge her own path, no matter what.

Chapter 12: Picking Up the Pieces

Rochelle woke up to the gray dawn filtering through the thin curtains of her small bedroom. The familiar sounds of the Richmond housing projects greeted her: distant sirens, the hum of early morning traffic, and the faint chatter of neighbors beginning their day. She took a deep breath and swung her legs over the side of the bed, determined to face another day of rebuilding her life.

The first step was finding a new routine. Rochelle enrolled in night classes at the local community college, determined to earn a nursing certification. She spent her days working part-time at a grocery store, saving every penny she could to eventually move out of the projects. It wasn't easy, but she was driven by a newfound sense of independence and the desire to create a better future for herself.

One morning, as she walked to the bus stop, she passed a group of women who were gossiping loudly. "Did you hear about Rochelle? Girl's trying to put her life back together after what happened with Josh," one of them said.

"Yeah, but can she really move on? Everyone knows her business," another added, her tone dripping with skepticism.

Rochelle kept her head high and walked past them without acknowledging their words. It stung to be the subject of their gossip, but she refused to let their judgment derail her progress. She was stronger than their idle chatter.

At work, Rochelle found solace in the routine of stocking shelves and helping customers. Her boss, Mr. Jenkins, noticed her hard work and dedication. "You're doing a great job, Rochelle. Keep it up, and you might find yourself moving up in this place," he said with a nod of approval.

"Thank you, Mr. Jenkins," Rochelle replied, her voice filled with gratitude. The compliment boosted her spirits, reinforcing her belief that she could rise above her circumstances.

During her night classes, Rochelle found herself immersed in the world of education. She soaked up the lessons, driven by the desire to prove to herself and others that she could succeed. Her classmates, many of whom had their own struggles, became a source of support and camaraderie.

One evening, after a particularly challenging class, Rochelle sat outside the school, reflecting on her journey. She thought about Josh and the dreams they had shared. The pain of their breakup and the miscarriage still lingered, but she also realized that those experiences had shaped her into a stronger, more resilient person.

"Hey, Rochelle," a voice called out. It was Malik, a classmate who often studied with her. "You wanna grab a coffee? We could go over some of those math problems together."

Rochelle smiled, appreciating the offer. "Sure, Malik. That sounds good."

As they sipped coffee at a nearby café, Malik shared his own story of overcoming adversity. His struggles with family and the streets mirrored Rochelle's in many ways, and their conversation gave her a sense of solidarity. She wasn't alone in her journey, and that realization brought her comfort.

In the following weeks, Rochelle continued to focus on her goals. She spent her evenings studying and her weekends volunteering at a local community center. Giving back to her neighborhood, despite its flaws, made her feel connected to something greater than herself.

But the challenges of moving on in a place where everyone knew her business were ever-present. One afternoon, as she walked through the projects, she spotted Josh leaning against a wall, talking to a group of guys. His leg was still in a brace, and he looked lost and disheartened.

Their eyes met briefly, and Rochelle felt a pang of sadness for what could have been. But she also knew that she couldn't let herself be pulled back into the past. She had to keep moving forward.

Later that evening, Rochelle sat on her bed, reflecting on her choices. She thought about the lessons she had learned from her relationship with Josh: the importance of self-worth, the dangers of losing oneself in another person, and the strength that comes from within.

She pulled out a journal and began to write, pouring her thoughts onto the pages. Writing became a form of therapy, a way to process her emotions and track her progress. She wrote about her dreams, her fears, and her plans for the future. The act of writing helped her to see how far she had come and how much further she could go.

As the days turned into weeks, Rochelle's confidence grew. She started to see herself not as a victim of her circumstances, but as a survivor. She was no longer defined by her relationship with Josh or the gossip of the neighborhood. She was defined by her resilience, her determination, and her ability to rise above adversity.

One evening, as she walked home from class, Rochelle stopped by the park where she and Josh used to dream about a better future. She sat on the old bench, looking out at the familiar scene. But this time, she felt a sense of peace. She had taken control of her life, and she was proud of how far she had come.

Rochelle knew that the journey ahead would still be challenging, but she was ready to face it. She had picked up the pieces of her life and was building something new and beautiful.

Chapter 13: A New Path

Rochelle stood at the edge of a new beginning. The dust of her tumultuous past with Josh was beginning to settle, and she felt a sense of clarity she hadn't experienced in a long time. The neighborhood, with its familiar sounds and faces, still held the shadows of her old life, but Rochelle was determined to carve out a new identity, one that was hers alone.

The first step was to focus on her own dreams and ambitions. Rochelle had always loved helping people, and with the encouragement of her night class instructors, she decided to pursue a career in nursing. The decision felt right, like a beacon guiding her through the lingering darkness of her past.

Enrolling in the community college's nursing program was both exhilarating and daunting. Rochelle walked through the halls, clutching her books tightly. The sight of other students, many younger and seemingly more confident, was intimidating. She took a deep breath and reminded herself why she was there.

In one of her first classes, Rochelle met Ms. Turner, an experienced nurse and one of the program's instructors. Ms. Turner was a formidable woman with a stern face that softened only slightly when she spoke about her passion for nursing. She noticed Rochelle's nervousness and pulled her aside after class.

"Rochelle, right?" Ms. Turner asked, her voice firm but not unkind.

"Yes, ma'am," Rochelle replied, trying to hide her anxiety.

"I can see you're serious about this. Nursing is tough, but if you're dedicated, you can make it. Just remember, it's not just about the skills. It's about the heart."

Rochelle nodded, feeling a surge of determination. "I'm ready to work hard, Ms. Turner. I want this more than anything."

Ms. Turner's nod of approval felt like a small victory. "Good. I'll be keeping an eye on you. Don't disappoint me."

Breaking away from the past wasn't easy. The neighborhood was a constant reminder of her history with Josh, and she often ran into people who still saw her as the girl defined by that relationship. The gossip had died down somewhat, but there were always whispers, always looks.

One afternoon, as Rochelle walked to the community center where she volunteered, she overheard a conversation between two women sitting on a stoop.

"She's trying to be a nurse now, can you believe it?" one woman said, her tone skeptical.

"Yeah, good for her, I guess," the other replied, her voice laced with doubt. "But you know how it is around here. The past has a way of catching up."

Rochelle felt a pang of anger but quickly replaced it with resolve. She was no longer living for their approval. Her path was her own, and she was determined to walk it with her head held high.

At the community center, Rochelle found unexpected allies. The staff and other volunteers were supportive and encouraging, recognizing her efforts and dedication. Mr. Williams, the center's director, took a particular interest in her progress.

"Rochelle, you're doing great work here," he said one day after a busy shift. "Have you ever thought about running some of the health workshops? You have a way of connecting with people."

Rochelle was taken aback. "Me? Run a workshop? I don't know if I'm ready for that."

Mr. Williams smiled. "You're more ready than you think. People here respect you. They see the changes you're making in your life. Use that to inspire others."

The offer was both thrilling and terrifying. Rochelle agreed, and soon she found herself leading workshops on basic health and wellness, drawing on her studies and her own experiences. The community's response was overwhelmingly positive, and for the first time, Rochelle felt like she was truly making a difference.

One evening, after a particularly successful workshop, Rochelle sat in the park, reflecting on her journey. She thought about the obstacles she had faced, the pain and betrayal, and the strength it had taken to keep moving forward. She was proud of how far she had come but knew there was still a long road ahead.

As she watched the sun set over the city, Rochelle felt a sense of peace. She had taken control of her life and was building something meaningful. The support she had found in unexpected places had given her the courage to dream bigger and to pursue those dreams with everything she had.

The streets of Richmond were still tough, and the challenges were far from over. But Rochelle was tougher, and she had found a new path, one that led to a future filled with promise and hope. She had learned to navigate the darkness and had discovered the strength within herself to shine brightly despite it all.

With each step forward, Rochelle felt herself growing stronger, more confident, and more determined to make a difference. She had found her purpose, and nothing could stand in her way. The streets might never forget her past, but Rochelle was no longer defined by it. She was carving out her own identity, and the future was hers for the taking.

Chapter 14: Facing the Truth

The streets had a way of bringing people back together, whether they were ready for it or not. As Josh hobbled through the neighborhood on his crutches, he was a shadow of his former self. The injury had ended his basketball dreams, and with them, his identity had crumbled. The attention he once thrived on was gone, replaced by a haunting loneliness.

Josh's thoughts were consumed by Rochelle. The girl he had betrayed, the girl who had believed in him more than anyone else. He had seen her around, watched her from a distance as she rebuilt her life with a strength he had never truly appreciated. And it was killing him inside. He had to talk to her, to try and make amends, even if it was too late.

One afternoon, Josh saw Rochelle walking home from her classes. Summoning his courage, he called out to her. "Rochelle! Wait up!"

Rochelle stopped, her heart pounding. She hadn't spoken to Josh since the hospital, and the sight of him brought a rush of emotions. Anger, sadness, a flicker of the love she once felt. She turned slowly, meeting his gaze.

"What do you want, Josh?" she asked, her voice cold but trembling slightly.

Josh limped closer, his eyes filled with regret. "I need to talk to you. Please, just give me a few minutes."

Rochelle crossed her arms, her defenses up. "Fine. Talk."

Josh took a deep breath, struggling to find the right words. "I know I messed up. I hurt you in ways I can't even begin to understand. I've been thinking about everything, and I just... I'm so sorry, Rochelle."

Rochelle's eyes flashed with anger. "Sorry? Do you even know what you're sorry for? You didn't just hurt me, Josh. Our baby, our future... you threw it all away."

Josh's face crumpled with pain. "I know, I know. And I hate myself for it. I was stupid and selfish. But I miss you, Rochelle. I miss us. Can we... can we try to fix this?"

Rochelle's heart ached. Part of her wanted to believe him, to give him another chance. But the wounds were still fresh, and the scars ran deep. "You think it's that easy? That you can just say sorry and everything will be okay?"

"No," Josh said quietly. "I know it's not easy. I know I have to earn your trust back. But I want to try. I want to be the man you deserve."

Rochelle shook her head, tears welling in her eyes. "You should have thought about that before you cheated on me. Before you ruined everything."

The confrontation was raw, their voices echoing through the empty street. They stood there, two broken people, trying to navigate the wreckage of their past.

Josh stepped closer, his eyes pleading. "Rochelle, please. I know I don't deserve it, but I'm begging you to give me a chance. Let me prove that I can be better."

Rochelle took a step back, her emotions swirling. She wanted to believe him, but the pain was too great. "I don't know, Josh. I don't know if I can ever forgive you."

Josh's shoulders slumped, defeat washing over him. "I understand. But I had to try. I had to tell you how sorry I am."

Rochelle looked at him, seeing the sincerity in his eyes. For a moment, she saw the boy she had fallen in love with, the boy who had shared her dreams. But then she remembered the betrayal, the heartbreak, and the loss.

"I need time," she said finally. "Time to figure out if I can ever trust you again."

Josh nodded, tears streaming down his face. "Take all the time you need. I'll wait."

As Josh walked away, Rochelle felt a mixture of relief and sadness. She had faced the truth, spoken the words that had been buried deep inside. But the path ahead was still uncertain.

That evening, Rochelle sat in her room, reflecting on the confrontation. She thought about her journey, the strength she had found within herself, and the new path she was forging. Forgiving Josh was a possibility, but she knew it couldn't be rushed. Trust was fragile, and it would take time to rebuild.

Over the next few weeks, Rochelle focused on her studies and her work at the community center. She poured her energy into helping others, finding solace in the act of giving back. The support from her classmates, her colleagues, and unexpected allies in the community helped her stay strong.

One day, as Rochelle led a health workshop, she felt a sense of purpose and fulfillment. She was making a difference, creating a future she could be proud of. And in that moment, she realized that her identity was no longer tied to Josh or their past. She was Rochelle, a strong, independent woman, capable of overcoming any obstacle.

Josh continued to reach out, sending messages of apology and hope. Rochelle read them, feeling a mix of emotions. She wasn't ready to forgive, but she wasn't ready to close the door completely either. The future was still unwritten, and she would take it one step at a time.

Chapter 15: The Final Decision

The weight of Rochelle's decision hung over her like a dark cloud, obscuring the path ahead. Each day, she weighed the pros and cons, replaying her conversations with Josh and reflecting on the journey they had shared. The streets of Richmond had seen them grow together, fall apart, and now stood as silent witnesses to her turmoil.

Rochelle spent her days immersed in her studies and work at the community center, hoping that the busyness would drown out her thoughts. But each evening, as she lay in bed, the decision loomed, demanding her attention. Could she truly forgive Josh? Could she trust him again after everything?

One afternoon, after a particularly grueling class, Rochelle decided to take a walk to clear her mind. The neighborhood was bustling with activity, kids playing in the streets, vendors shouting their wares, and the familiar sounds of life in the projects. She walked to the park, the place where she and Josh had once dreamed of a better future.

Sitting on their old bench, Rochelle closed her eyes and let the memories wash over her. She thought about the good times, the laughter, and the dreams they had shared. But she also remembered the betrayal, the heartbreak, and the pain of losing their baby. Her heart ached with the weight of it all.

"Rochelle?" a voice called out, breaking her reverie. She opened her eyes to see Mrs. Jenkins, the kind shop owner, standing nearby.

"Hey, Mrs. Jenkins," Rochelle replied, managing a small smile.

Mrs. Jenkins sat down beside her, her eyes filled with understanding. "You look troubled, child. What's on your mind?"

Rochelle sighed, the words spilling out before she could stop them. "It's Josh. He wants to make things right, but I don't know if I can trust him again. I don't know if I can forgive him."

Mrs. Jenkins nodded, her gaze distant as if recalling her own past struggles. "Forgiveness is a powerful thing, Rochelle. It's not about forgetting what happened, but about finding peace for yourself. But trust... that's something that has to be earned."

Rochelle looked at her, searching for answers. "How do I know if I'm making the right decision?"

Mrs. Jenkins placed a hand on her shoulder, her touch comforting. "Only you can know that, child. You have to listen to your heart and decide what's best for you. Don't let anyone else's expectations guide you."

Rochelle nodded, her mind clearer but still conflicted. She thanked Mrs. Jenkins and continued her walk, the old woman's words echoing in her mind. She needed to make a decision, not just for herself, but for her future.

That evening, Rochelle sat in her room, her journal open on her lap. She wrote down her thoughts, the pros and cons, her fears and hopes. As she wrote, a sense of clarity began to emerge. She knew what she needed to do.

The next day, Rochelle called Josh and asked him to meet her at the park. He arrived quickly, hope and apprehension written on his face. They sat on the bench, the tension between them palpable.

"Josh, I've thought a lot about what you said," Rochelle began, her voice steady. "I appreciate your apologies, and I believe you're sincere. But I need to be honest with myself and with you."

Josh nodded, bracing himself for her words. "I understand."

Rochelle took a deep breath. "I can't go back to how things were. Too much has happened, and I need to move forward with my life. I need to focus on my dreams and my future."

Josh's face fell, but he nodded, his eyes filled with sadness. "I understand, Rochelle. I really do. I'm just... sorry it took me so long to realize what I had."

Rochelle reached out, taking his hand. "I hope you find your way, Josh. I really do. But I need to do this for me."

They sat in silence for a moment, the reality of their parting settling in. It was a bittersweet moment, filled with regret and a glimmer of hope for the future.

The decision had been made, and as Rochelle walked away, she felt a sense of relief. It wasn't an easy choice, but it was the right one for her. She needed to focus on her path, her goals, and her healing.

The community reacted to Rochelle's decision with a mix of surprise and respect. Some admired her strength, while others questioned her choice. But Rochelle knew she couldn't let their opinions sway her. She was forging her own path, and she needed to stay true to herself.

Josh, on the other hand, faced a different reality. Without Rochelle, he had to confront his own demons and figure out how to rebuild his life. The streets of Richmond were unforgiving, but he was determined to find his way, to earn back the trust and respect he had lost.

As Rochelle walked through the neighborhood, she felt a sense of empowerment. She had faced the truth, made a difficult decision, and was ready to embrace the future. The challenges were far from over, but she was stronger now, more determined than ever to create a life she could be proud of.

The streets of Richmond were tough, but so was Rochelle. She had made her final decision, and with it, she was ready to move forward, leaving the past behind and embracing the promise of a brighter tomorrow.

Chapter 16: Redemption and Regret

The streets were a living testament to resilience and survival, and Rochelle was determined to carve out her own legacy of redemption. She had made her decision, severing ties with Josh to focus on her future. Now, it was time to turn her pain into purpose, to transform her experiences into a force for positive change in her community.

Rochelle threw herself into her work at the community center, channeling her energy into helping others avoid the pitfalls she had encountered. She began organizing workshops on health, education, and personal empowerment, drawing from her own life lessons to guide her sessions.

One afternoon, Rochelle stood before a group of young women, their faces a mixture of curiosity and skepticism. She took a deep breath, her heart pounding, and began to speak.

"I know what it's like to feel trapped," she said, her voice steady but filled with emotion. "To think that your circumstances define you. But I'm here to tell you that you can rise above it. You can make better choices and build a future you're proud of."

The room was silent, the young women hanging on her every word. Rochelle shared her story, the highs and the devastating lows, emphasizing the importance of self-worth, self-love and the power of education.

As she spoke, she saw a flicker of hope in their eyes, a glimmer of belief that maybe, just maybe, they could change their paths. It was in these moments that Rochelle found her redemption, using her pain to uplift others.

Meanwhile, Josh's journey was one of profound regret. Losing Rochelle had been a wake-up call, forcing him to confront the consequences of his actions. With his basketball career in ruins and his relationship shattered, Josh found himself at a crossroads.

Determined to make amends, Josh began volunteering at the community center as well. It was a humbling experience, facing the people who had once looked up to him and seeing the disappointment in their eyes. But he knew this was part of his path to redemption.

One day, as he was helping to organize a charity event, Josh ran into Mr. Williams, the center's director. Mr. Williams looked at him with a mixture of sternness and compassion.

"Josh, you've got a lot to make up for," Mr. Williams said. "But I believe people can change. It's up to you to prove that."

Josh nodded, determination etched on his face. "I will, Mr. Williams. I'm not going to let my past define me."

His journey was not easy. The neighborhood had a long memory, and trust was not easily regained. But Josh worked tirelessly, mentoring young boys, sharing his story as a cautionary tale, and showing them the importance of making better choices.

One evening, Rochelle and Josh found themselves working side by side at the community center. The tension between them was palpable, but there was also a shared understanding of their respective paths to redemption.

"Rochelle," Josh began, breaking the silence. "I know I've hurt you more than I can ever make up for. But I want you to know that I'm trying to change. To be better."

Rochelle looked at him, her expression softened by the passage of time and the shared goal of helping their community. "I can see that, Josh. And I respect it. We both have our own journeys now."

They continued their work, an unspoken truce between them. Rochelle focused on empowering the young women she mentored, helping them to see their potential beyond the confines of the projects. She saw herself in their eyes and felt a deep responsibility to guide them toward a brighter future.

Josh, on the other hand, poured his energy into coaching basketball, using the sport as a tool to teach discipline and teamwork. He found solace in helping others, slowly rebuilding his reputation and finding a sense of purpose beyond his past mistakes.

Their efforts began to ripple through the community, creating a sense of hope and possibility. Rochelle's workshops grew in attendance, and the young women she mentored started to believe in their own potential. Josh's basketball program became a safe haven for boys looking for guidance and a way out of trouble.

As Rochelle and Josh walked their paths of redemption, they found that their shared experiences, though painful, had given them a unique perspective and the ability to make a real difference. Their community, once filled with whispers of judgment, began to see them as symbols of resilience and change.

One evening, after a particularly successful community event, Rochelle and Josh stood outside the center, watching the sunset over the city. The streets of Richmond, with all their challenges and hardships, had become the backdrop to their stories of growth and redemption.

Rochelle turned to Josh, a hint of a smile on her lips. "We've come a long way, haven't we?"

Josh nodded, his eyes reflecting a mix of regret and hope. "Yeah, we have. And there's still so much more we can do."

In that moment, they both understood that their paths, though separate, were intertwined in their commitment to making a difference. The journey of redemption and regret was ongoing, but they had found a way to channel their past into a force for good.

The streets of Richmond were still tough, but Rochelle and Josh were tougher. And together, they were helping to build a future filled with hope, resilience, and the promise of positive change.

Chapter 17: The Championship Game

The air was electric with anticipation as the day of the championship game finally arrived. The entire community buzzed with excitement, the streets of Richmond teeming with people discussing the upcoming event. For many, the game symbolized more than just a sports event; it was a beacon of hope and a testament to the resilience of those who had fought hard to make it happen.

Banners and posters adorned the neighborhood, and the local gymnasium, usually a place of routine and practice, had been transformed into a vibrant arena. The bleachers filled quickly, the noise level rising as friends, family, and neighbors came together to support their team. The championship game was a big deal, a chance for the community to rally together and momentarily forget their troubles.

Josh sat on the edge of the bleachers, his eyes fixed on the court. His leg still bore the scars of the injury that had dashed his own dreams, but he had come to terms with it. Today, he was here not as a fallen star, but as a mentor, a supporter, and a symbol of redemption. He watched the young players warming up, their faces alight with determination and excitement, and couldn't help but reflect on what could have been.

Rochelle arrived with a group of young women from the community center, their excitement infectious. She had spent weeks preparing them for this moment, teaching them about the importance of dreams, resilience, and supporting one another. As she settled into her seat, she felt a sense of closure wash over her. She had come a long way, and watching the game with her mentees felt like the perfect culmination of her journey.

The game began with a burst of energy, the players moving with a fluid grace that spoke of countless hours of practice and dedication. The crowd roared, every basket met with cheers, every missed shot with groans. The gymnasium pulsed with a rhythm that echoed the heartbeat of the community itself.

Josh found himself lost in the game, the memories of his own time on the court flooding back. He remembered the thrill of the competition, the rush of adrenaline, and the camaraderie of his teammates. But he also remembered the mistakes, the betrayals, and the pain of losing everything. Sitting here now, he realized how far he had come. The game might have been his dream once, but life had taken him on a different path—one that was just as important.

During halftime, the crowd mingled, and Josh spotted Rochelle across the gym. Their eyes met briefly, and he gave her a nod, a silent acknowledgment of their shared history and the paths they had taken. Rochelle returned the nod, her heart lighter than it had been in years. She had found her purpose, her strength, and she was proud of the woman she had become.

The second half of the game was even more intense, the score neck and neck. The crowd was on the edge of their seats, every play a potential game-changer. Rochelle cheered loudly, her voice blending with the chorus of support from the community. She glanced at the young women beside her, their faces filled with awe and excitement, and felt a surge of pride. She was helping to shape their futures, to show them that they could rise above their circumstances.

As the clock ticked down to the final seconds, the tension was palpable. The home team had possession, and the star player, a young boy Josh had been mentoring, dribbled down the court. The crowd held its breath as he made his move, darting past defenders with skill and precision. With a final, determined leap, he released the ball, and the gym erupted in cheers as it swished through the net just as the buzzer sounded.

The home team had won the championship, and the crowd surged onto the court in a wave of celebration. Josh watched with a mixture of pride and nostalgia, feeling a sense of fulfillment that had been missing for so long. He had played a part in this victory, even if he wasn't the one on the court.

Rochelle stood with tears in her eyes, her heart swelling with joy. The game was a victory not just for the team, but for the entire community. It was a testament to the power of hope, determination, and the unbreakable spirit of those who refused to give up.

As the celebrations continued, Josh made his way through the crowd and found Rochelle. They stood face to face, the noise of the crowd fading into the background.

"You did good, Josh," Rochelle said, her voice filled with sincerity.

"So did you, Rochelle," Josh replied, his eyes reflecting a newfound respect and admiration. "We've come a long way."

They shared a moment of understanding, both realizing that their journeys had brought them to this point. The past was behind them, and the future was filled with endless possibilities. They had both found redemption in their own ways, and now it was time to move forward.

As the sun set over Richmond, the community continued to celebrate their victory. Rochelle and Josh stood together, watching the scene unfold with a sense of peace and closure. They had faced their demons, found their strength, and were ready to embrace whatever came next. The streets of Richmond were tough, but so were they, and the championship game had proven that they could rise above anything.

Chapter 18: Closure and New Beginnings

The streets of Richmond were waking up to a new dawn, the echoes of the championship game still fresh in everyone's minds. The community had celebrated their victory with a fervor that transcended the sport itself. For Rochelle, the game marked a pivotal moment in her life—a point of closure and the beginning of a new chapter.

Sitting on her porch, Rochelle gazed out at the neighborhood that had shaped her. The familiar sounds and sights of the projects were both comforting and haunting, a reminder of the hardships she had endured and the lessons she had learned. She thought back to the days when she and Josh had been inseparable, dreaming of a future that seemed just out of reach. The betrayal, the heartbreak, and the loss of their baby had all been devastating, but they had also been catalysts for her transformation.

Rochelle had grown stronger, more resilient. She had faced her demons and emerged with a sense of purpose that had been absent in her younger years. Her work at the community center had become a beacon of hope for many, and she had found fulfillment in helping others navigate the challenges of the streets.

The community was slowly moving on, each person carrying their own memories of Rochelle's journey. Some remembered her reign with admiration, others with skepticism. But Rochelle had learned to rise above the opinions of others, focusing instead on the impact she could make.

"Rochelle, you've done so much for us," one of the young women she mentored said, sitting beside her on the porch. "You've shown us that we can be more than our circumstances."

Rochelle smiled, her heart swelling with pride. "Thank you. But remember, it's your strength and determination that will carry you forward. I'm just here to guide you."

The girl nodded, her eyes shining with determination. "We won't let you down."

As the girl walked away, Rochelle felt a sense of peace. She had planted seeds of hope and resilience, and she knew that the community would continue to grow and thrive. Her own journey, filled with tumult and triumph, had led her to this point. She was at the top of her game, but she remained vigilant, knowing that the streets never truly let go.

Rochelle's plans for the future were ambitious. She wanted to expand the community center's programs, offering more resources for education, health, and empowerment. She had dreams of starting a scholarship fund for young people in the neighborhood, giving them opportunities she had never had. Her vision extended beyond Richmond, hoping to inspire similar initiatives in other struggling communities.

One evening, as she was preparing for a meeting with potential donors, Josh approached her. He had been working tirelessly at the community center, his own path to redemption intertwining with hers. They had found a new dynamic, one built on mutual respect and a shared commitment to positive change.

"Rochelle, can we talk?" Josh asked, his voice tentative.

Rochelle looked up, nodding. "Sure, Josh. What's on your mind?"

He took a deep breath, the weight of his past mistakes still evident in his eyes. "I just wanted to say thank you. For everything. You've shown me what it means to truly give back, to find purpose beyond ourselves."

Rochelle smiled, a sense of closure washing over her. "You've come a long way, Josh. I'm proud of the man you're becoming."

Josh nodded, a flicker of hope in his eyes. "I owe a lot of that to you. I know we can't change the past, but we can build a better future."

As they stood together, watching the sun set over the neighborhood, Rochelle felt a sense of completeness. Her journey had been fraught with challenges, but it had also been filled with growth and transformation. She had faced her fears, found her strength, and was ready to embrace the future.

Rochelle's plans were already in motion, and she was determined to see them through. She knew the road ahead would be tough, filled with obstacles and setbacks, but she was prepared. The lessons she had learned in the streets had armed her with the resilience and determination needed to succeed.

As the night descended on Richmond, Rochelle reflected on her journey. She thought about the hardships, the betrayals, and the moments of despair. But she also remembered the victories, the growth, and the lives she had touched. She had come full circle, finding her place in a community that had once seemed determined to break her.

Rochelle stood at the top of her game, a beacon of hope and resilience. But she never forgot the lessons of the streets. She knew she had to stay vigilant, always watching her back, ready to face whatever challenges came her way. The streets of Richmond were tough, but so was she, and she was ready to continue her journey with strength and determination.

As she walked back inside, Rochelle felt a sense of closure and new beginnings. She had faced the darkness and emerged stronger, and now she was ready to light the way for others. The future was filled with promise, and Rochelle was determined to seize every moment, knowing that she had the power to shape her destiny and inspire others to do the same.

In Loving Memory of
Joseph Lewis Fitzgerald

Don't miss out!

Visit the website below and you can sign up to receive emails whenever Rachael Reed publishes a new book. There's no charge and no obligation.

https://books2read.com/r/B-A-WXARB-DEJPD

BOOKS 2 READ

Connecting independent readers to independent writers.

Did you love *Championship Bad*? Then you should read *Can't Turn a Hoe Into a Housewife*[1] by Rachael Reed!

[2]

In the gritty streets of the city, where loyalty is tested and danger lurks around every corner, Can't Turn a Hoe into a Housewife dives deep into the underbelly of urban life. Erica, a seasoned escort with a sharp mind and a guarded heart, dreams of escaping the fast life and finding something real. But in a world where money rules and trust is scarce, her journey ain't easy.

When Erica crosses paths with Quan, a man with a genuine heart and a promise of love, she sees a glimmer of hope. But leaving the game ain't simple, especially with a ruthless pimp like Lil Ron, who

---

1. https://books2read.com/u/4XdEN1

2. https://books2read.com/u/4XdEN1

ain't about to let his top girl go without a fight. As Erica tries to walk the line between her old life and a new beginning, Lil Ron tightens his grip, turning their lives into a deadly game of cat and mouse.

Can't Turn a Hoe into a Housewife is a tale of love, betrayal, and survival in a world where the streets don't play fair. With a dark, raw tone and a cast of characters struggling against their circumstances, this story is packed with twists, drama, and the harsh reality of street life. As Erica fights to break free and find redemption, the stakes get higher, and the danger becomes all too real.

In this urban fiction thriller, the line between right and wrong blurs, and every choice comes with a price. Will Erica escape the life that's bound her, or will the streets claim her for good? Get ready for a cliffhanging ride through the hood, where love ain't always enough to save you from your past.

Also by Rachael Reed

Codefendant
Codefendant
Once a Cheater
Once a Cheater
Passport Bro
What Happens in Prison
Preference
Sprinkle Sprinkle
Championship Bad
Street Exodus
Street Exodus
Street Royalty
Pawns of Power
SIS
Cartel Bloodline
Get Money Girls
Skip the Games
Til Death Do Us Part
Backpage Hustle
Link in Bio
The Virgin and The Kingpin
A Gangsta's Heart
Boosters

Can't Turn a Hoe Into a Housewife